Mistaken for a Call Girl

Charlie Daye

Other Titles by Charlie Daye

Curse Breaker's Series

The House
The Colonial
The Reservation

The Hunter's Series

The Gypsy's Dance

Angel Stories

Her Last Request

Stand Alones

Butterfly

Novellas

The Portrait (Part One)

This is a work of fiction. Any resemblance to persons or places known, unknown, living or dead, named or unnamed was purely coincidental. This work may not be shared, copy or distributed without the authors express permission. Cover photo credits - Image ID: 18878770. 123rf.com.

©2013 Charlie Daye

Dedication

For Mr. McKinley…

Without your "misunderstanding" this story would have never existed.

ONE

My name is Thalia Tyme. Yes, that is my name and no, I'm not making it up. I'm twenty-five years old, with a degree in hotel management and hospitality, am currently single or at least I was before this whole misunderstanding occurred. I also used to be human.

I was on my way to an interview at the prestigious Hotel Loret for an opening they had for Hotel Manager. I was so excited I could hardly contain myself. I had been dreaming of working at Hotel Loret for as long as I could remember. You might think that's strange but I have a weird obsession for old hotel's that are reminiscent of old Hollywood – when men like Humphrey Bogart lit up the screen and leading ladies like Audrey Hepburn were the epitome of what Hollywood glamour should be. It was the kind of place where everyone wanted to be seen and you just knew that if you pressed your ear to the wall it would whisper all its secrets to you.

Wanting to impress whomever it was I was set to interview with, I decided on a black pencil skirt with a red silk camisole and the matching black suit coat. I pulled out my favorite pair of 1940's style stilettos and pinned my flaming red hair in to a twist on the back of my head. I wasn't a big fan of make-up but did decide to adorn just a tad bit of eyeliner and mascara around my eyes to bring out the green in them. The color in and of itself wasn't very dark or very bright. As a matter of fact, my eyes were a rather pale shade of green that was almost nondescript. They were so bland in color that if you passed me on the street you might not notice they were green at all.

I arrived at the hotel fifteen minutes before my scheduled interview. I was told I would be meeting with a Mr. Smith at six. Sighing deeply, I put my hand on the handle of the glass doors and pulled.

I was always overwhelmed at the beauty that was Hotel Loret. The entire inside of the hotel was done in off white limestone, modern art adorned the walls, a giant chandelier hung over the center of the lobby and the furniture was a cross between fifties elegance and modern day chic. I walked over to the front desk and was warmly greeted by the hotel concierge, "Good afternoon madam. How may I be of assistance?"

I tried to control my excitement as I responded, "I have a six o'clock appointment with Mr. Smith."

"And your name?" he asked.

"Thalia Tyme," I replied.

As controlled as his features were, I could tell that my name had caught him off guard. He smiled, "Please have a seat Ms.… Tyme. I'll let Mr. Smith know you're here."

I thanked him before moving off to sit in the lobby. A few minutes later, the concierge approached me, "Ms. Tyme?"

I looked up, "Yes?"

"Mr. Smith said he's going to be a few minutes longer and asked that you await him in the lounge. Shall I show you the way?"

I shook my head; I'd been here enough times that I probably knew the layout of the hotel better than most of the staff, "No thank you. I'm familiar."

The concierge nodded, "Of course."

I rose and made away across the lobby to the lounge. The lounge was beautifully done with wood floors, cherry tables and white leather chairs. It had a fully stocked bar and just enough lighting to give off a romantically sexy feel. I took a seat at a table in the corner of the room giving me the advantage of being able to see who was coming in and out of the lounge. I had no idea what Mr. Smith looked like but was sure there weren't going to be many men walking in the lounge searching for me.

I must have been sitting there for at least twenty minutes before the most beautiful man I had ever seen walked in. He had jet black hair that was neatly styled and just touched the bottom of his shirt collar. He was well over six feet tall with the body of a professional athlete - not too big, not too small but just right. His shoulders were broad and tapered down into a trim waist. The most startling thing about him was his eyes. They sparkled like dark green emeralds and stared at me with such intensity that I felt the urge to squirm in my chair. My heart began to race as he made his way to my little table in the corner.

The physical attraction I felt was immediate, however, I was there for an interview and if this happened to be the yet unknown Mr. Smith, I wanted my first impression to be memorable.

He smiled at me and it wasn't the kind of smile that said 'hello'. It was the kind of smile that a man gives a woman when he knows exactly how the night is going to end – with you naked in his bed.

Not wanting to sit and have him tower over me, which wouldn't have made much difference since I was only five feet tall, I stood up. Yes, it was ridiculous but it did make me feel better. He stopped just on the other side of the table, "Ms Tyme?"

I swallowed. Lord help me… please don't be Mr. Smith. "Yes?"

He held out his hand as if waiting to escort me from around the table. I stared momentarily at the offered hand before placing my trembling hand in his. "Please forgive my tardiness. I was tied up with another appointment."

I smiled. Of course he was Mr. Smith. Why would he not be? "No problem. I'm just glad you could squeeze me in."

"I'll always make time for a beautiful lady," he remarked.

I thought the comment was a tad bit inappropriate since this was a job interview but decided to let it slide for the moment. Yes, I know I'd lusted after him from the moment he walked in the room but at least I didn't verbalize my thoughts.

Once I was around the table and standing next to him, he placed my hand around the crook in his arm and began to escort me out of the lounge. Again, I thought this was a little strange but then again maybe Mr. Smith was just really old fashioned. I just wouldn't realize how old fashioned until later.

We walked back through the lobby and into an elevator where Mr. Smith took out a key and inserted it into a key whole on the elevator panel. Curious, I asked, "Why the key?"

He smiled, "My offices are private. This way, only staff with the right clearance has access to the highest floors of the hotel."

I nodded my understanding.

We rode the rest of the way in silence until we reached what I assumed was the top floor of the hotel. Ever the gentleman, he let me leave the elevator first, then once again took my hand and wrapped it around his arm. We finally stopped at the end of a very long hallway where he ushered me into a tastefully sophisticated office. The entire back wall of the office was a giant window covered in sheer panel curtains. The carpet was charcoal grey, the desk was a glossy black and situated on the other side of the room was a set of white leather sofas with a glass coffee table between them.

I took a seat in one of the chairs before his desk as he made his way over to a bar in the corner, "Can I offer you a drink?"

I shook my head, "No thank you."

He poured himself an amber colored liquid over a few ice cubes and turned to look at me. He once again had that look that promised wicked things to come. I nervously straightened out my skirt, "So… do you have any questions for me?"

He smirked, "Not really."

"You don't?" I asked confused.

He tossed back his drink and set the glass back on the bar, "Let's not be coy Ms. Tyme. We both know why you're here. Is conversation really necessary?"

I frowned, "Of course we know why I'm here… for an interview. I just assumed you'd want to know more about me."

He chuckled and made his way back to his chair, "Is that the story you were asked to come in here with? Very well." He sat down and leaned back in his chair. "So, tell me about your experience."

I smiled, "I graduated from the University of Phoenix with my degree in Hospitality and Hotel Management. I spent my summers working in various hotels in different positions so that I would have a better understanding of how a hotel functioned at different levels."

"And how many positions have you held Ms. Tyme?"

"Not many. Perhaps five at the most? I wanted to make sure that I had a good understanding of the primary functions of hotel operations – like housekeeping, front desk, room service, etc."

"Ever have any extremely demanding customers when you delivered to their rooms?" he asked with an amused look on his face.

"Oh! All the time! Especially when they didn't like how their food was delivered," she replied. "Sometimes people can be so anal about things like that."

He chuckled, "Yes, they can be."

He rose from his chair and walked around the desk until he was standing behind me. The minute he was out of sight was the minute everything changed. The hair at the nape of my neck stood on end. I was suddenly terrified – feeling like the fly that got caught in the spider's web. I practically jumped out of my chair when Mr. Smith trailed his finger down the side of my neck.

I spun placing my butt against his desk and a protective hand over my throat, though I had no idea why I'd done that. "What are you doing?"

He smiled predatorily at me, "I'm hungry and horny and I think this game has gone on long enough."

I stepped further away from him intent on making my way towards the door but before I could even clear the desk he pounced and I found myself pinned to his desk with my skirt hiked up to mid-thigh. His groin was pressed against mine and could I tell how happy he was to be there. He gripped my chin in his hand and angled my head away from him exposing my throat. I tried clawing at his hand but when that didn't work I decided to beg, "Mr. Smith… please don't."

He turned my face back to him so that I could take in his glowing eyes and elongated teeth. "Come now Ms. Tyme. Surely you knew that you'd been sent here to satisfy my needs."

Fear overrode logic and reason. He looked every much the vampire but vampires weren't real, right? Wrong. Doing the only thing I could think of, I thrashed against him and screamed at the top of my lungs.

TWO

"A feisty one. I am definitely pleased," he remarked.

My throat became hoarse from all the screaming and all my thrashing seemed to do was push my skirt higher up my body which seemed to suit him just fine. He had moved his hand from my chin to my neck and held it firmly using only his thumb to maneuver my head around. Spreading my legs further apart, he pushed my black thong to the side and began rubbing slow circles around my clit. I stopped screaming long enough to gasp, "Please don't."

He smiled down at me, eyes glowing and fangs glistening in the light, he inserted a single digit into my body testing my limits before inserting a second. "Nice and tight," he commented. "I'll have to remember to send my thanks to the agency later."

I squeezed my eyes shut pushing the tears out of the corners of my eyes which had started to pool. I tried fighting him off again but all he did was squeeze just enough on my throat to make spots appear in my vision. It also didn't seem to be helping my case that I could feel liquid heat running from between my legs and my hips kept pushing up to meet his fingers. I settled for wrapping both my hands around the wrist of the hand that held my throat and pleaded softly once more, "Mr. Smith… please let me go. I promise not to tell anyone what you are."

He angled my head to the right and leaned down to run his tongue up the length of my neck. When he reached my ear he whispered, "You're a good actress. I'll give you that but what I really want right now is to be inside you. Both here," he said licking my neck, "and here," he said inserting a third finger into my soaking channel.

I moaned. I just couldn't help it. Despite my best efforts to not be turned on, this man…er… vampire was doing a damn good job of nearly having me climax right on his desk- and he knew it.

He inhaled deeply. "I can smell your fear and your arousal. It's quite a potent combination."

Between the three fingers pumping my sex and his thumb circling my clit I was on my way to a sure fire melt down. I tightened my grip on his wrist and closed my eyes as the most amazing orgasm I'd ever experienced ripped through my body. My muscles clamped on to his fingers as the rest of my body convulsed. It was also at that moment that another strikingly handsome man walked into the office with an overly curvy woman on his arm with dyed red hair and breasts so large you knew they were fake. He looked from me to Mr. Smith and said, "Roman? Who's this?"

Mr. Smith, aka Roman, withdrew his fingers from my still pulsating core and licked my juices off of them, "The call girl from the escort service."

The other man shook his head, "No. This is Natalia from the escort service. I have no idea who you have there."

Roman turned his attention back to me still lying on his desk. The glow from his eyes began to fade as understanding sank in as to what he'd just done. His predatory look fell away and was replaced by a look of shock and horror. "Oh my God. Your name is Thalia not Natalia," he said immediately releasing me and stepping away. "I'm so sorry. I just assumed that the concierge got your name wrong and when he said you had red hair… well" he said gesturing towards Natalia. "I just assumed."

I slowly got up off the desk and made my way to the door. I was more than humiliated. I was terrified. I still had tears running down my cheeks not to mention the obvious signs of my release running down my legs.

The other man turned to Roman and looked just as shocked as Roman did, "This is Thalia Tyme? Your interview for the hotel manager position? Christ Roman, what were you thinking?"

Roman took a step toward me. He reached for me but didn't touch me, "Thalia I'm so sorry. I didn't know."

I wiped my face, "But I tried to tell you. You just didn't listen." Trembling, I took a step back, "I need to go."

The other man stopped me. "Thalia, I'm Victor. I own Hotel Loret with Roman. We were really looking forward to interviewing you. Your references were impeccable and we thought you'd make an excellent candidate for the position. I'm so terribly sorry about this and perhaps I don't have a right to ask but will you consider coming back again tomorrow to speak with us about working here?"

Was he out of his damned mind? Not only did I just get sexually assaulted but I was sexually assaulted by a freaking vampire! I shook my head, "I don't think so."

Victor gestured for Natalia to go take a seat on the couch, which she did, before he focused his full attention on me. He approached me slowly as if he was afraid any sudden movements might scare me off; which, if truth be told, they probably would have. He took one of my hands in his and wiped away a stray tear. I looked into his eyes and was startled by the brilliance of the blue tones. "Thalia, are you sure because if that is truly the way you feel I'm afraid we'll have to erase your memory of this night. There is no way we can let you leave here knowing that vampires exist."

I jerked back away from him but he didn't release me. His grip actually became tighter to the point of bordering on pain. A whimper escaped my lips, "Please I just want to go home."

A growl came from behind me with a warning, "Victor."

Victor looked at Roman, his eyes beginning to pulse, "What Roman? This little fuck up was your doing. Be hopeful that I might be able to salvage this because I'd hate to have to kill her."

That really got my attention. I struggled a little more and this time Victor released me. I took a step back and bumped into the very solid chest of Roman Smith. He wrapped his arms protectively around me which surprisingly, I was okay with. At least he hadn't offered to kill me… yet.

"I will handle this Victor. Why don't you take Natalia to your office and I will join you as soon as I'm done here."

"Very well Roman but make sure you do. We can't have a human running around town with the knowledge that we exist." Victor looked at Natalia, "Come sweetness."

Natalia rose from the couch and moved to join Victor. She glanced in my direction with a look of almost sympathy before she walked out the door with Victor.

"I'm very sorry about this Thalia," he whispered in my ear.

Something about the intimacy of our position and the manner in which he spoke to me had my body aching for his touch again. I tilted my head back so that I could look up at his face, "Please don't hurt me Roman. I swear I won't tell a soul. I just want to go home."

He brushed his thumb across my cheek, "You are so lovely." He leaned over and captured my mouth in a kiss that was so hot I was almost positive my lips were about to melt right off my face. When he pulled away from the kiss, his eyes were glowing, "I'm going to take you home Thalia and when you wake up tomorrow you won't remember anything about what happened here tonight – only that your interview was rescheduled for tomorrow night at six."

I remember staring into his eyes and him touching my forehead. He said, "Sleep." And I did.

THREE

I woke the next morning feeling strangely… alone. I gazed around my room. Everything was in its proper place; I was even wearing my favorite pajamas. Although, admittedly, I couldn't tell you how I got into them. I rolled over and buried my face into the extra pillow on my bed and inhaled deeply. I'm not sure what I was expecting to find but it definitely wasn't the scent of my laundry detergent. It was as if I expected to smell a man's cologne. I had the vaguest memory of being intimate with a man or was it being held by a man? The memory was fleeting like a dream you desperately want to cling to but can't quite reach for.

Sighing, I rolled out of bed. As much as I would have loved to spend all day in bed trying to figure out what I was missing, I had errands to run and an interview at Hotel Loret.

The day seemed to drag. Or maybe it was just because I was anxious about my interview. I spent an entire hour staring at the clothing in my closet trying to figure out what the hell to wear. I couldn't understand what my problem was. It's not like it was my first interview but for some reason I had butterflies dancing in my belly like they would if I was about to go on a first date with a really hot guy that I'd been lusting over for a while. I pulled out my favorite pencil skirt then frowned as something fought to come to the forefront of my mind. Whatever it was it was making me very uncomfortable so I hung the skirt back up and decided on a really stylish belted dress. It was white, form fitting and sleeveless and had a thin black belt to accent it. The neckline was high and straight and it looked very professional. I decided on a pair of black and white spectators to complete the look.

The next hour was spent in the bathroom trying to decide how best to manage my hair. For some reason the thought of wearing it up was extremely unappealing. I had no desire to have my neck exposed for this little interview. So, I brushed out my hair, which reached to the middle of my back and curled it all in big loose curls. After applying a little bit of makeup, I looked myself over and decided this was as good as it was going to get and headed out to my interview.

I arrived at the hotel well before my appointed time. I informed the concierge that I was there for an interview and told him I'd be at the bar waiting. Ten minutes later a strikingly handsome man approached me. He had dark brown hair and stunningly blue eyes. He was dressed impeccably in a very expensive Italian suit. "Ms. Tyme?" he asked.

I smiled, "Yes?"

He held out his hand, "Victor Granger, owner of Hotel Loret."

I jumped off my stool and accepted the offered hand, "Mr. Granger! I had no idea I'd be meeting with the owner this evening."

He smiled looking relatively pleased, "I'm glad I could surprise you. If you'll join me, my partner and I would like to ask you a few questions?"

"I'd love to," I replied, walking with him to the elevator.

We talked casually about nothing as we rode the elevator and waited for the elevator doors to open. We continued our journey down an extremely long hallway until we stopped in front of a set of closed doors. He opened the doors and ushered me inside. The office was stylish with its black and white themed décor. Mr. Granger gestured to the bar, "Please, help yourself to a drink while I fetch my partner Mr. Smith."

I smiled, "Alright, thank you. Would you like me to make you a drink as well?"

Victor smiled, "That would be lovely thanks. Scotch on the rocks please."

Not a minute later, I heard the door reopen. I turned to greet who ever had entered and was ensnared in a matching set of emerald colored eyes. My heart began to beat a mile a minute and I had no idea why. It seemed to be a mixture of fear and arousal – which honestly, was an odd pairing.

"Ms. Tyme, I'd like you to meet my partner Mr. Smith."

Mr. Smith approached me rather slowly and held out his hand. I accepted it while still staring into his eyes. The minute we made contact a very vivid memory rose to the surface in my mind… of this man bringing me to climax right on the desk in this very room. I gasped and whispered, "Roman."

His eyes widened in surprise. When I tried to pull away he gave a small shake of his head, which for some reason I knew to listen to immediately. Trying to hide my discomfort, I smiled, "It's nice to meet you Mr. Smith."

His features relaxed at my understanding of the situation, "Hello Ms. Tyme. Please, call me Roman."

I could do this. I could make it through one stinking interview with a man who had brought me to the best orgasm of my life or at least I hoped I could. It wouldn't be weird. Right? Smiling, I said, "I'm sorry that I didn't think to make you a drink. It never occurred to me to ask Mr. Granger what you wanted."

Roman smiled, "It's alright. I'm very capable of making my own."

Victor smiled, "Shall we get started?"

"Absolutely," I replied.

Roman sat behind his desk and Victor and I took the seats in front of it. It was Victor who spoke first. "You have a very impressive resume Ms. Tyme. I love the fact that you opted to try out various jobs in several hotels. What made you do it?"

"How can you run a hotel if you don't know how to do every job there is? It just made sense," I replied.

"Your fellow co-workers speak very highly of you," Roman admitted. "Is there any reason you never accepted a permanent job with one of them?"

"Truthfully, I'd been holding out to work here. I'm completely in love with this place. I love the old glamorous Hollywood feel the place has. To me it just feels like the kind of place where everyone who wants to be seen should be. I bet if these walls could talk they'd have some amazing stories to share," I replied.

I couldn't help but look down at Ramon's desk then up at the man himself. He was looking hungrily at me – that's the only way to describe it. I found myself needing to look elsewhere as the blush rose up my cheeks.

We spent the next hour talking about the hotel, my experience and the ideas I had in mind if I were to be offered the job. They both seemed very receptive and I took it as a good sign. As the interview came to an end, I shook both their hands and thanked them for their time. Victor walked me back down to the lobby, "Thank you for coming in today Ms. Tyme."

I smiled, "I should be thanking you. I'm not sure if you have any other interviews set up but I would really love the opportunity to work with you both. I think the hotel is gorgeous and has great potential." I shook his hand, "I hope to hear from you soon."

Victor smiled, "Have a good evening Ms. Tyme."

"You as well."

FOUR

As far as I could tell the interview had gone well but I still couldn't shake the feeling that I was missing something. What was it with that memory of Roman and his desk? To the best of my knowledge, I couldn't remember ever meeting him but the explosive memory and the look in his eyes as he stared at me said otherwise. Was it a repressed memory that I was purposely trying to forget? Was it wishful thinking? That thought made me laugh, "That's one hell of an imagination you've got there girl if that's the case."

Deciding for some much needed ME time, I cleaned up my mess in the kitchen from dinner and took a glass of wine with me to the bathroom. I wanted to soak in the tub and think about absolutely nothing – especially the set of matching emerald eyes that kept haunting my every waking moment. I sat on the side of the tub waiting for it to fill and was just about to slip into it when there was a knock at my front door. I retied my robe and checked the clock. It was almost ten. Who in the world would be knocking on my door this late in the evening?

I made my way back to the living room and opened the door. It never occurred to me to check the peep hole first but the minute I saw my visitor I was wishing I had. "Roman?"

He smiled as his eyes ran from my head to my blue colored toe nails, "Can I come in?"

I frowned adjusting my robe. I suddenly felt extremely under dressed, "I'm not sure yet."

"I'm not going to hurt you Thalia," he replied softly.

"Isn't that usually what the bad guy says to give a false sense of safety?" I asked.

Roman chuckled, "Point taken. I just want to talk to you."

I chewed my bottom lip. I was having some serious issues at the moment. One being my overwhelming need to jump this man where he stood and the other being the need to run and hide under my bed which I thought was very strange. I stepped back and opened the door wider, "Can we make this quick? I was about to indulge in some much needed me time."

He stepped into my house and I closed the door behind him. When I turned around he had me pinned to the door, "How much do you remember?"

I swallowed. His close proximity was making my heart beat way too fast. "What do you mean?" I rasped.

"You recognized me today Thalia. It takes a special woman to be able to undo what I did to you."

"What did you do to me?" I whispered.

He leaned in close, wrapping his hand around my throat, "I laid you on my desk and fucked you with my fingers until you came."

I closed my eyes and shuddered at the onset of memories that flooded my brain. I remembered… everything.

He licked my neck, "You remember don't you?"

"Yes," I replied shakily.

"What am I?" he asked.

"Vampire," I replied.

He nibbled my ear, "Does that scare you?"

"Yes."

"Do I arouse you?"

I considered saying no but figured he might be able to sense my arousal just like he had the day before. So I decided the truth was best, "Yes."

"I tried to make you forget Thalia. I was trying to protect you."

"From who?" I asked breathlessly.

He slid his hand down the front of my robe, manipulating my nipple into a tight peak before continuing south towards my sex. Pushing my robe open, he exposed my naked body to his greedy hand. He gently searched the folds of my sex, stroking, caressing, playing… until he pushed back and slipped a finger into my body. I moaned.

"I was trying to protect you from us… from me."

"Why?" I asked, riding his finger.

"Because from the minute I saw you, I wanted to bury myself so deep in your body that no one would be able to tell where you began and I ended," he replied.

I threw my head back against the door as he pushed another finger into my body and dug my nails into his shoulders. "I should be afraid of you," I panted. "But all I seem to want to do is fuck you."

He kissed me hard and deep, "Then allow me to fuck you and then I will explain everything because right now I can't seem to focus on anything other than making you cum."

That mini speech alone had me ready to climax where I stood, "Yes, yes, yes… Please!"

Fortunately for both of us, I was not prone to motion sickness. Vampires move faster than the eye can see and before I blinked an eye we were lying in my bed naked. He was poised above me and without a moments hesitation he sunk deep into my body making me cry out. He rode me hard and fast bringing me closer and closer to the edge of insanity. His kisses were deep and thorough. It felt as though he was trying to crawl into my body from both ends – claiming me, marking me.

"Thalia," he called through gritted teeth.

I opened my eyes to stare into his. They were glowing bright green, "I'm going to sink my fangs into your flesh and take my fill."

You'd think that would have completely freaked me out but it didn't. I found the idea to be a complete turn on and simply said, "Yes."

Roman grinned, displaying his elongated fangs and just as I reached my peak… he struck. I screamed out, part pain, part pleasure. My body convulsed around his. I felt the hot stream of his seed fill my womb as the essence that was me filled his. I was flying on the most amazing high I had ever experienced and had no desire to come down.

Roman finally pulled away and licked my neck lovingly, "You taste like the sweetest honey."

I laid there, my body boneless, "I don't think I'll be able to walk for at least a week. That was beyond amazing."

Roman chuckled and pulled slowly from my body. His absence was dually noted by a slight wince of pain and an immense gaping hole of emptiness. He rolled onto his back and pulled me into his arms, "There is much I need to tell you about us but it will take some time. Do you want to talk now or would you like to rest for a while?"

"Us?" I asked. "Are you referring to your people or you and I?"

He smiled and stroked his hand up and down my back, "Both."

FIVE

I was both exhausted and exhilarated. I had just had the best sex of my life with a man I didn't know, who also happened to be a vampire. Both my sex and my neck ached from the double penetration. You'd think I'd feel bad about having sex with someone I'd only just met but since this wasn't technically our first time together I decided I could let it go. Yes, yes, I know I was crying like a baby yesterday and half terrified out of my mind but now that he was here in my bed... none of it seemed to matter anymore. Strange? Perhaps.

"I can almost hear the wheels turning in your head Thalia. What are you thinking about?"

I propped my head on his chest, resting my chin on the back of my hand, "Well, let's see... you practically raped me yesterday after showing your *real* self to me which I might add scared the shit out of me. Now, I'm lying in bed with you living in the after glow of the most amazing sex of my life and I'm starting to wonder if something's wrong with me. Why am I not running out the front door screaming at the top of my lungs for someone to call the cops?"

Roman chuckled, "There is absolutely nothing wrong with you Thalia."

"Then why aren't I running?" I asked again.

"Because you're mine," he replied matter of factly.

"Excuse me?" I asked arching my brow.

He ran his hand down the side of my face sending shivers down my spine. "Thalia, are you familiar with compulsion?" he asked.

"To an extent," I replied. "I mean, I've watched the Vampire Diaries."

He laughed, "We'll go with that." He paused. "Vampires have many abilities, one of those being compulsion or the power to make you do whatever they want you to do. I used that gift on you yesterday in hopes that you would forget about our little… misunderstanding."

I laughed. I couldn't help it, "Misunderstanding? Is that what they're calling it these days?"

He yanked on a piece of my hair and smirked, "Shoosh woman. I'm trying to tell a story here."

I bit my lip to contain my laughter, "I'm sorry, please continue."

"Normally, our powers work perfectly and the human is none the wiser but every once in a while a human be it male or female is able to pull out of the compulsion and once they do, none of our gifts work on them ever again. When that occurs, the human is usually taken and mated with a vampire and eventually turned into one themselves."

"And what if said human doesn't want to be turned into a vampire," I asked quietly.

Roman shook his head, "Do not ask me that question."

I sat up remembering a comment Victor made. It made my skin run cold and all the color drain from my face, "You kill them."

"Occasionally," he replied.

"And the other times?" I asked.

"You remember Natalia?" he asked.

"I'd become a vampire hooker?" I asked shocked.

Roman winced, "We don't refer to them as such."

"And how exactly do you refer to them?" I asked. "Dinner? Dessert?"

"Don't be ridiculous Thalia. Any human taken by the agency to… service us… is treated with the utmost care and respect. They're given posh accommodations, make more money than most fortune 500 CEO's and want for nothing."

I frowned, "So, my options are become a vampire bride, a call girl or die?"

Roman sat up and took my hands in his, "Would being mated to me for all eternity really be that bad?"

I ran my eyes from the top of his head to the tips of his toes. He was sheer perfection right down to the slowly rising package between his legs. I subconsciously licked my lips wondering how much of that oversized package I could get in my mouth.

He chuckled, "See something you want sweetheart?"

I blushed at being caught staring and placed a pillow over his crotch, "Sorry, couldn't help myself."

"It's yours for eternity if you want it."

I sighed, "But what if we hate each other a month from now? What if we decide that oops we made a mistake and want to be with other people? What if I turn out to be a horrible vampire?"

He laughed, "First of all, there's no such thing as a horrible vampire. Once turned, vampirism becomes as natural as breathing. Second, when you're turned, you are done so by your mate, which ensures a life long bond that will only strengthen over time with the constant sharing of blood and sex. And lastly, vampire relationships are not that much different from human ones. We will fight, we will disagree but we will always come back to each other."

I crossed my arms over my chest, "So what, we'd only feed off each other for the rest of eternity?"

Roman shook his head, "No, we'd still need humans to feed."

"Right and you'd what, fuck them all like you attempted to do to me yesterday?" I asked sarcastically.

"Well," he said pursing his lips. "Sex and blood usually do co-mingle in our world."

I'm not sure why that totally pissed me off but it did. I'm mean it's not like I'd made a decision either way yet, but we are talking about potentially being married and he's telling me that he'd be sleeping with other people? What the fuck ever! "Not gonna happen... so just kill me now!"

Roman arched his brow in surprise, "What?"

"Listen," I said unable to keep the anger from my voice. "I don't wanna be a call girl and honestly I don't wanna die either but I also don't want to be involved with someone who thinks it would be ok to go sleeping around with every woman he sinks his fangs into. So unless you have a fourth option you haven't told me about yet let's just get it over with."

Roman looked at me for a moment before bursting into a fit of laughter, "Oh, Thalia. You are a gem. If the only thing keeping you from being my mate is the thought of me sleeping with other women we can change that."

I dropped my face in my hands and groaned, of course.

He pulled my hands away and tilted my head up, "Thalia?"

"Yeah?" I said sighing deeply.

"Do you want to be my mate?"

"I don't know yet," I replied.

He smiled, "Are you sure?"

I shrugged, "To be honest, I'm not sure of anything anymore. Yesterday morning I was content with my life and the possibility of finally landing my dream job. Now, I'm faced with a decision that will alter my life forever and no matter what I decide there'll be no turning back."

Roman cupped my face and kissed me softly, "What do you think about when I'm near you?"

"Being in your arms," I replied honestly.

"And when I'm not around?" he asked kissing the side of my mouth.

"I'm lonely."

He began pushing me back down on the bed, "And when I kiss you?"

"I want more…" I whispered.

He slid his hand between my legs and caressed me gently, "And when I touch you?"

I closed my eyes and groaned, "I want you inside me."

"Like this?" he asked sliding home.

I reached up to kiss him, fisting my hands in his hair. "Just like that," I purred.

His hips flexed slowly, "Then how can you deny that we belong together?"

"I don't even know you," I protested weakly.

He smiled as he ground his pelvis into mine, "We have eternity to get to know each other Thalia."

"Eternity?" I asked completely lost in the feeling of Roman between my legs and my overwhelming need to be close to him.

"Yes, Thalia," he whispered. "Say yes."

I closed my eyes and bared my neck, "Yes."

SIX

Do you know that feeling you get when you wake up extremely hung over? Now, add that to feeling like you have the flu and just got hit by a Mac truck and you'll know exactly how I felt the moment I opened my eyes.

I was completely disoriented and had no idea where I was. The room I was in was not familiar to me and to be honest I'm not exactly sure how I got there. I was lying on a bed dressed in black sheets and a white comforter. The pillows at my back were a mixture of the two colors as were the curtains in the room.

Movement caught in the corner of my eye had me turning my head achingly slow to see who was in the room with me. My vision was still a little blurry so I stared for a moment or two until my visitor came into focus. "Victor?" I rasped. My throat felt like sand paper.

He smirked, "Thalia. How are you feeling?"

I closed my eyes and swallowed trying to alleviate some of the dryness in my throat, "Like someone beat me with a baseball bat."

He moved towards the bed, "You'll feel better after your first feeding."

Feeding? I thought. How will eating anything other than Tylenol make me feel better? I raised my hands up to my face and groaned at the effort it took, "Where am I?"

"Roman's."

I jumped slightly at the sound of his voice being so close to me. I couldn't tell by the way he looked at me if he was happy or angry and knowing that he'd made mention to kill me when we first met wasn't helping. "Are you going to kill me now?" I asked.

Victor tilted his head and studied me, "Why would you ask that?"

"You did mention it when we first me," I reminded him.

He smiled, "True but that was before I knew what you were and now that you've been claimed by Roman you're safe."

"I'm what?" I asked.

"How much do you remember Thalia?"

"About what?" I asked.

"About everything," he replied.

I sighed, "I remember the day we all met and Roman mistaking me for a call girl. I remember my interview with the two of you and Roman coming over to my place that night. Then nothing till I woke up here."

Victor nodded his understanding, "Do you remember the conversation you had with Roman about your options?"

I nodded then regretted it when pain shot through my neck, "Yeah."

"Do you remember him biting you?"

"Uh, yeah, a couple times actually."

Victor sat down on the bed, "Do you understand, Thalia, that Roman turned you?"

I swallowed. I kind of figured that's what would've happened when I bared my neck to him but was content living in my little bubble of denial for the moment. "Yeah. I got that."

"He's also claimed you as his mate," he added.

"Yeah, we talked about that too," I replied. "Speaking of... where is that charming man of mine? Shouldn't he be here nursing me back to health or something?"

"He'll be back soon. He just stepped out to feed."

"What?" I asked not liking the idea one bit. Especially since he and I had never come to terms or an agreement on sex and other people. I threw the covers off me despite my body's protesting, "Where is he?"

Victor's eyes widened in surprise, "What do you think you're doing?"

"I'm going to go find my *mate* and ring his neck. Now, where is he?"

Victor moved to stop me, "Thalia, you really need to rest. Roman will be back soon, I promise."

I looked at Victor and growled surprising both of us… who knew! "I want to see him now!"

Victor shook his head and smiled, "Very well."

I stood on shaky legs and started slowly for the door, "Where?"

Victor opened the door for me and pointed down the hall, "Third door on the left."

Normally, I would have loved to explore the beauty that was Roman's home but I was too pissed off at the moment to even consider it. I made my way both painfully and slowly down the hall until I came to the third door on the left. I almost burst into tears when I heard a woman moaning on the other side of the door.

I flung the door open and stepped inside. What I saw was not what I was expecting. Roman stood behind a woman with short blonde hair, his arms wrapped tightly around her waist, fangs deep in her throat, eyes closed. The woman looked like she was having the most amazingly orgasmic experience of her life, which was all self inflicted because she had her skirt hiked up to her waist and her hand tucked into the front of her panties, fingers moving quickly.

The sound of the door banging against the wall had Roman opening his eyes. He withdrew his fangs from the woman's neck and all but tossed her aside and rushed to my side. The look on his face was a cross between anger and concern, "Thalia! What are you doing out of bed?"

He reached me the instant my legs gave out beneath me. Had he not been there to catch me I would have fallen to the floor. Tears started to pool in my eyes, "Victor said you were feeding and I just assumed…"

Roman cradled me to his body and kissed my head, "My sweet girl. I told you I wouldn't take another to my bed if you opted to be my mate."

"No you didn't," I sniffed. "We never got that far in the conversation."

Roman threw his head back and laughed, "True, but the idea was implied my sweet."

I dropped my head on his shoulder, "Are you done feeding?"

"I'm good for the moment. How are you? Are you hungry? Should I call for someone for you?" he asked concerned.

I wrapped my arms around his neck and buried my face in his shoulder, "No, just take me back to bed."

SEVEN

Roman carried me back to his room. Victor was still there sitting casually in a wingback chair sipping a glass scotch. After placing me on the bed and recovering me, Roman turned to Victor, "Why the hell did you let her out of bed? She could barely stand let alone walk."

Victor shrugged, "She said she wanted to ring your neck. Who am I to stand in the way of love?"

Roman threw up his hands, "Seriously Victor? She needs rest and food…"

"And you," I croaked out.

Roman turned to me, his features softening, "You have me my sweet girl."

I patted the mattress next to me, "Come lie with me."

He smiled and moved to sit on the bed, "Sweetheart, I need to get you some food. It'll help with your transition."

I went to shake my head and winced when pain shot through me again. You figure I'd learn after the first time. "I'm not hungry."

"Here," Victor said handing Roman a glass of dark red fluid. "It's fresh."

I grimaced, "I'm not drinking that."

Roman accepted the glass and pushed it towards me, "You need to Thalia. It'll make you feel better."

"But it's blood," I protested.

"And you're a vampire," Victor reminded me.

Sighing dramatically, I reached for the glass. I brought the glass to my nose and sniffed, prepared to upchuck at the idea of ingesting someone's life force but when the aroma hit my nose it was all I could do not to lick the glass clean.

I emptied the glass in two seconds flat then closed my eyes and savored the feel of the warm liquid sliding down my throat. Yum! When I opened my eyes, both Victor and Roman were staring at me like proud papas. With just one glass, I was already feeling one hundred percent better. I held up the glass and grinned, "More please."

After several more glasses of blood, Roman finally agreed to let me up out of bed to take a much needed shower. I'd discovered that I'd been going through the transition for three days and although I didn't smell, the former human part of me felt dirty.

Roman's bathroom was like every woman's wet dream. There was a walk in shower large enough for five people with shower heads coming out everywhere. The bathtub was a massive Jacuzzi tub that I couldn't wait to try. I turned on the shower to start the water heating before I walked back into the bedroom. Roman and Victor were talking quietly. I almost felt bad interrupting them… almost. "I need clothes and toiletries, please."

They both turned to me and stared.

"What?" I asked.

"Stunning," Victor commented.

"Agreed," Roman added.

I looked down and myself and laughed, "Are you guys talking about me? Because I highly doubt I look anything but disgusting."

Roman walked over and directed me to the nearest mirror. It took me a minute to realize what it was I was looking at. My bright red hair had become darker and richer, my pale green eyes had turned into an electric green – sharp with multi-faceted contrasts and my skin was alabaster perfection.

I reached up and touched my own face, "Whoa."

"My thoughts exactly," Roman agreed. "Not that you weren't perfect before."

I laughed, "Nice save Romeo."

Roman turned to Victor, who was still staring at me from the bedroom, "Could you excuse us Victor? I'd very much like to have a private moment with my wife."

"Your wife?" I asked surprised. "When was the wedding?"

Roman turned my head to show two faint puncture wound scars on my neck, "The night I did this."

I touched the marks gently, "So, the night you turned me I became your wife?"

He nodded, "Yes."

I turned to look at him, resting my butt up against the counter, "Alright, here's the deal. I'll give you the vampire wedding thing, I'll even accept that we're mated for all eternity but you've gotta give me something in return."

Roman smiled, "Anything."

"I want my ring," I grinned.

EIGHT

It took me two weeks to get acclimated to my new vamp powers and it was on the three week anniversary of my being turned that Roman surprised me... twice. First, he gave me the most beautiful ring I had ever seen. It was a three carat princess cut engagement ring with a matching wedding band. He even bought himself a diamond encrusted wedding band to match mine. Second, after placing said ring on my finger and I placing his on his finger, he opened the door and ushered me to a delicious looking man that if I had to guess, was about the same age I was. He had blond hair and blue eyes and a body to die for. I looked at Roman questioningly.

"I want you to feed from the vein my sweet," he replied.

My eyes rounded, "Oh, I don't know about that."

Roman tsked at me, "You'll have to learn sometime."

Sighing, I dropped down on our bed, "You won't leave me will you? You'll stay while I feed?"

"Of course I will." He turned to the man, "Phillip."

Phillip nodded and pulled off his shirt exposing a field of rippled abs to my hungry eyes. Oh boy! I thought.

Roman sat down next to me and reached for my hand. He brought me to sit between his legs, arms wrapped around my waist and whispered in my ear, "It's okay to touch him sweetheart, just no sex. That's the rule, remember?"

I nodded, "I remember."

"Phillip, if you will…" Roman instructed.

Phillip smiled at me as he knelt down before me, "Would you like me facing you or turned away from you?"

"I...I'm not sure," I stuttered.

"If I may, my sweet?" Roman asked.

I nodded, "Please."

"Phillip, why don't you face away? I think forward facing may be a little too intimate for her first time."

"Of course Roman," Phillip agreed.

Turning around, Phillip stood on his knees with his back to my knees and pushed back until I was forced to spread my legs so he could rest between them, which was a little unnerving since I was wearing a dress. I looked back at Roman; he simply smiled and kissed me on the cheek. I turned my attention back to Phillip. I wasn't exactly sure where to place my hands, so I settled for resting them on his shoulders. I leaned towards his neck; I could see his vein dancing around beneath his skin as if it was calling to me. I opened my mouth hoping that my fangs would descend on their own. I shouldn't have been worried. With a dull ache, they popped out and I struck fast and sure. It was instinct, just like Roman said.

Phillip's blood was like a fine wine as it hit my tongue and slid down my throat. It was better than anything I'd been given to date. Fresh from the vein was definitely better than poured from a glass.

I closed my eyes and ran my hands all over Phillip's body. His skin was soft and smelt of soap and man. His muscled abs quivered under my touch and I found that both exhilarating and erotic. I slid forward placing my groin against his back. I was extremely horny and now fully understood the need for sex and blood. I was trying to behave. I really was but Phillip's soft moans of pleasure were not helping my cause.

There was a slight jarring motion and I opened my eyes to find that Phillip had popped open his button fly jeans and pulled out his throbbing erection. He ran his hand up and down it rapidly. The sight had liquid heat pooling between my legs.

Roman moved up behind and pulled my dress back to my waist. He slid his hand into my panties and licked my neck, "You're wet my sweet. Do you like what you see?"

I released Phillip's neck and turned to Roman. He kissed me reverently, licking Phillip's blood off my lips. "Yes," I whispered.

Roman took my hand and pushed it down the front of Phillip's body, "Touch him."

I froze, "No."

Roman nibbled at my neck sending chills down my spine, "You can touch him Thalia. You just can't sleep with him."

I shook my head, "I can't."

"Why?" he asked softly.

"Because I couldn't stand it if you touched another woman that way," I replied.

Roman moved his fingers expertly around inside my panties until I began panting, "I would never do anything with another woman without your permission first Thalia. I would not hurt you that way. You have my word. Now, touch him. Show him how much you appreciate what he's given you." He grabbed my hand and moved it back towards Phillip's waiting erection. I hesitated only briefly before I wrapped my fingers around him and began pumping my hand up and down his length – then I sunk my fangs back in to his neck.

Phillip's moans of pleasure were like music to my ears and Roman's hand in my panties was amazing but that was not what I really wanted. Without my having to ask, Roman moved away briefly then returned lifting me up and pushing my panties to the side before pushing me down on to his body. I purred happily. The minute I felt Phillip's release, I let him go and focused my attention on Roman.

I lifted my dress up over my head and lost the bra. It was at that point that Roman instructed Phillip to leave the room and I found myself on my back with Roman positioned above me. He licked the remnants of Phillip's blood off my mouth without missing a single stroke. I wrapped my legs around his hips and cried out with every thrust. I had a moment's notice before Roman reared back and struck, sinking his fangs deep into my throat sending me over the edge of sexual bliss.

We lay wrapped in each other's arms for several minutes before I found the sense to be embarrassed about groping another man in front of my husband. I could feel the burn in my cheeks and tried to turn away from him. He stopped me.

"Why are you trying to turn away from me?" he asked softly.

I buried my face in his shoulder, "Because I did the one thing that I would never forgive you for doing."

Roman laughed, "Sweetheart, if you'll remember correctly, it was I that moved your hand."

"I know, I know but still," I protested.

He cupped my face and tilted my chin, "Thalia, I only did that so you could get the full understanding of how we feed. Now, please keep in mind that I will not have you doing that when I'm not around nor without my permission, as I would never do that to you."

Really?" I asked hopeful.

"Really," he replied. "I'm finding the idea of sharing you with anyone – be it human or vampire – to be very unappealing."

I wrapped myself around his body and squeezed, "Thank you."

He laughed, hugging me to his body, "How thankful are you?"

I popped my head up off his chest and grinned, "Very."

He propped his hands behind his head and grinned, "Show me."

NINE

It has been six months since Roman and I have been married, at least in vampire terms. We put my little house on the market and moved all my things into his place. Feedings have gotten a lot easier and I stopped needing to touch my donors while I feed. Victor went ahead and hired me for the hotel manager position. By then it was just a formality for the rest of the hotel staff. Roman and I were almost inseparable and both he and Victor liked the idea of having another vampire run the hotel in their absence.

My introduction into vampire society went a lot easier than anyone expected. Although, there were murmurings that the call girls weren't happy about losing the sexual god that was Roman Smith. Victor thinks it's funny and always jokes about that leaving more women for him. Roman says he can have them.

I still see my friends and family on occasion but Roman has already informed me that eventually we'll have to move away for a while. People will start to get suspicious when they notice we don't age.

Roman and I did talk about growing our family. Apparently vampires can have children but since he and I have eternity together, neither one of us really feels the need to start procreating right away. We'd much rather spend a few hundred years getting to know each other better. Although I have to admit, I think I know him pretty well physically.

I'm pretty sure I'm in love with the sexy vamp. I haven't told him yet but I think he already knows. We haven't discussed it in any detail yet because the idea scares the crap out of me but there are days when we're together and I'm thinking about how much I love him and he'll look up at me and smile and I'll hear his voice in my mind whispering, "I love you too." For now, I'm going to continue to live in my little bubble where I can pretend that my thoughts are still my own.

Since I took over running the hotel, there have been no more "misunderstandings" when it comes to guests vs. call girls. Sometimes I think Roman still feels bad about what he did to me the day we met but I think for him the end result was worth it.

How do I feel you ask? Hmmm… I've got the job I've always wanted, I'm forever young and beautiful, I'm married to the man of my dreams who just so happens to be a vampire and I'm happier than I ever thought I could be. Would I change any of it if I could? Absolutely not. As a matter of fact, Roman and I occasionally play around in his office reliving the day we first met. Except now… I'm always the willing call girl.

Printed in Great Britain
by Amazon